I WANT TO BE SUPER MESSY

Cam R. Pearce

ISBN 9781702847377
Independently published

Publisher's Note

This is a work of fiction. Names, characters, places, dialogues, and incidents are either the product of the author's imagination or used fictitiously. Any resemblance with actual persons, living or dead, business establishments, events or locales is

DEDICATION

To Mum, Dad, and Pippa

(who are not at all like Matt's family)

CONTENTS

ACKNOWLEDGMENTS

I want to thank my teacher, Mr. Johnston, my friends at school, and Pippa, for reading my manuscript and giving helpful feedback.

I would also like to thank my parents for encouraging me to make my book.

Without Auntie Esther and Auntie Delyth, my book would be full of errors!

Thank you, Kristina, for doing all the beautiful pictures.

And finally, I want to thank my Grandma, Mimi, for suggesting I write a book during school holidays instead of just being glued to technology. Without you, I wouldn't have this book to share with all my new readers!

PART 1

I finally decided I had **ENOUGH**!

Enough of being teased all the time and being called names. Enough of being pushed around. Enough of feeling small.

Before my decision to become the messiest kid in Grade 4, my Mum had turned me into a super-clean mega-embarrassment for all at school to make fun of.

After you read Part One, you will agree with me that my life was no laughing matter at all — at least not FOR ME!

Everyone else at school thought it was hilarious to make fun of me. I was their favorite teasing target.

Ordinary parents don't seem to spend much time trying to keep their kids from getting dirty. They clean them up and wash their stuff.

But some parents, like my mother, for example, spend all their attention and effort on turning their kids into the most unnatural state of tidiness in the whole universe.

The first part of this book is about my life of misery as a super-clean and spotless school student, so sparkly and shiny that even the sun could not compete with me.

I was the perfect poster boy for grownups who have nothing better to do than think up new ways of torturing their kids with soap and water.

After you have read Part One, you will understand **WHY** I **NEEDED** to make a change.

Part Two is about how I used different ways to get grimy, filthy, messy, and absolutely revolting.

Not just ordinary dirty, but extraordinary dirty, messy, and icky.

I wanted to turn my world into a world of muck and grubbiness. I wanted to gross out everyone around me.

I was hoping Mum would eventually **WISH** to see me just covered in the everyday type of dirt that hangs on to ordinary kids.

Then I wouldn't get teased anymore at school. My life would be normal, and I could enjoy it for a change. That is what I was hoping for.

Part 3 is about what happened after I turned into the messiest kid in school. It wasn't exactly what I had expected.

ABOUT ME —
A SHORT SNAPSHOT

You most definitely have never heard of me before.

Yet.

But I'm sure you will one day because I will be the most famous football player in the world when I grow up.

My name is Matt, and I am nine years old. Apparently, I am just an ordinary kid — according to my school reports.

I have brown hair and some wobbly teeth — two, to be precise.

People say I am skinny. They say my arms and legs are too long, and I also have long feet. They don't know that this the best thing when you play football. You can run faster and stretch further to get to the ball.

Football is called soccer in Australia; in case you didn't know.

I will tell you more about where I live in

the next chapter.

Mum and Dad want me to get a proper education. Dad wants me to become a lawyer, but Mum wants me to be a doctor.

I keep telling them that this is not what I want. Being a doctor and seeing blood or sitting in an office all day and talking to criminals is just not my dream.

I want to be like Lionel Messi from FC Barcelona. He is the best soccer player of ALL TIME. When I grow up, I will be like him.

For my birthday, Dad gave me the FIFA 18 soccer game to play on PlayStation. I play it every day to get my skills up, and I practice with my ball as much as I can at home, on our lawn, and in the living room, much to Mum's frustration.

Dad takes me to the Golden Square District Soccer Club on Wednesdays after school and to their games every Sunday morning during the soccer season. I freeze to death on these mornings, and my legs are wobbly from the cold. That makes it challenging to play.

For Christmas, my auntie gave me an FC Barcelona shirt with the number 10 on the back. That is Messi's squad number at FC Barcelona. I try to wear it wherever I go, except school, and even use it as my pajama top — until Mum takes it away into the wash because she says it is dirty.

For now, I try to keep Mum and Dad happy, and I go to school every day, just sitting there waiting for the bell to go so that I can go out and play soccer during recess.

I feel like I am the odd one out in our family and at school, and you will soon know why.

MY PERFECT FAMILY

I live in an ordinary town in Australia. In case you don't know, Australia is a big continent in the middle of the Southern

Ocean, just off Antarctica.

Most people come here on a plane, but some old people come on big cruise ships. They usually leave again after a few days.

Our town is at the seaside, and I live in an ordinary house with Mum and Dad and my sister Isabelle.

Dad is an architect, and he designed our house. Dad calls it ordinary; Mum thinks it is fancy.

Outside, we only have a patch of grass. Mum calls it the 'The Lawn'. I only use it to practice soccer skills because it is not big enough for anything else.

Mum and Dad believe they are perfect in everything, but I know that Dad picks his nose when he is driving to work, and Mum sometimes farts. She never owns up to it and always blames it on Grump, my dog. Mum and Dad think Isabelle is the perfect princess, but she bullies me all the time when they are not there.

Isabelle is four years older than me. Most of the time, she is a real pain.

She is a copy of Mum, telling me off for everything:

"Don't touch me with your grubby hands!"

"Don't go into my room, Slimy!" That's what she calls me.

"Don't contaminate my stuff with your fourth-grade germs. Get away from me, you filthy creature!"

Yesterday I collected a handful of dog hair from Grump's dog bed and put it under her pillow. This morning she complained to Mum.

"My bed stinks, this filthy dog has been sleeping in my bed again."

Dad works in the city and drops me off at school every morning.

Mum is obsessed with having everything clean and tidy. And I mean — EVERYTHING!

For her, that means every piece of furniture must be in the same place every day — not one millimeter to the left or right.

I am not allowed to build a cubby house with sofa cushions and blankets. That's why I like to go to sleepovers at Owen's. His Mum doesn't mind cubby houses in the living room.

Mum has a routine about everything.

Most of her routines are about keeping me and my stuff clean. I cannot understand why she always picks on me. It's all about:

"Wash your hands!"

"Brush your hair!"

"Brush your teeth!"

"Have you washed your ears?"

"Take your dirty socks to the laundry!"

"Leave your muddy shoes outside!"

Mum is afraid of germs. She disinfects everything she can think of:

1. The bathroom
2. The toilet — every day!
3. The fridge
4. My soccer boots
5. My school bag
6. Grump's dog bed
7. Grump's food bowl
8. Grump's water bowl.

Everything stinks of her cleaning chemicals.

Mum says we will all get sick from germs if she doesn't do that.

I can't see it makes a difference. Owen's Mum never disinfects anything, and Owen is not as sick and snotty as often as me.

GRUMP — MY BEST FRIEND

Grump is my dog. He is big and brown and has shaggy fur. I think Dad called him Grump because he is the opposite of grumpy. He is the happiest dog ever when he sees me.

Dad let me have Grump because he says that every boy needs a dog. I totally agree with that, but Mum thinks it is outrageous and unhealthy.

Grump likes to sleep on my bed when nobody is looking.

I usually let him because I love him. He is very comforting. I don't mind when he drools on my pillow.

His drool is spectacular. He can make slimy white drool that hangs from his lips halfway down to his chest, especially when he is watching me eat something.

He is also a gigantic farter, and he burps a lot.

When Grump sleeps, he snores as loud as Dad.

Mum kicks Grump out of the house if she catches him on my bed.

"OUT! OUT! You are a revolting, disgusting canine, get OUT into your doghouse!"

She gets into a real flap about him being in my bed.

"Dogs have germs and fleas and worms. I don't want him in my house."

She takes him to the vet every five minutes to make sure he doesn't make me sick.

Last time the vet said we should look after Grump's teeth better.

That gave me an idea, but first I want to tell you about my school.

THE START OF AN ORDINARY SCHOOL DAY ….

My school is called Meadow Vale Middle School. Dad brags to his friends about how good the school is, but I think it is a bit more ordinary than he believes.

The kids in there are just ordinary like me, some even more ordinary. I admit there are quite a few that are better than me in everything, sports, and math and reading. You get the picture. I think I am somewhere in the middle of everything — except soccer.

The best thing about the school is that it has a soccer pitch and a school garden.

Obviously, you can work out why I like the soccer pitch. Of course, I made it into the school soccer team. In fact, I am in the A-team. We train twice a week, Monday and Thursday. We play a game each Saturday morning against the B-team and other schools.

I like the school garden because at home we don't have a garden like this with garden beds for vegetables and fruit trees. We also have a school pond with reeds and fish in it. There are some frogs too, but they usually hide from us.

I only have two friends at school, Cameron and Dillon. They are in the picture at the top of this chapter. Cameron is the one with the black hair.

Everyone calls me 'Spick'. That's for 'Spick and Span' which apparently means super neat and tidy. Sometimes they also call me 'Spotless'. They make fun of me because of the way I look. I hate that.

It's probably because every morning I come to school looking super 'immaculate'.

That is what Mum calls this look. 'Immaculate'.

I had no idea what that word means. I had to look it up on Google. I found it means 'Spotless'.

Which means I look like an ad in the school uniform shop window.

Never a speck of dirt or a spot of food on my shirt.

My shoes — always black and shiny like a mirror.

My pants — always the right length.

Never a button missing from my blazer.

Worst of all, everyone's making fun of my hairstyle.

The hairdresser cuts it the way grandma likes it. Grandma takes me to the hairdresser every month. The hairdresser and grandma are friends and very old-fashioned. They are both fans of a singer called Elvis. I don't know any tracks of him, but they say he was the greatest ever.

If it were my choice, I wouldn't have that hairstyle. I would have it like Lionel Messi.

One of my biggest tormentors at school is Patrick. Unfortunately, he also plays soccer. Luckily for me, he is on the B-team. He is even taller than I am but twice as wide and a lot heavier. Because he is so big, the coach picked him to be the goalie.

Patrick totally ignores me most of the time. He calls me 'SCRAWNY', or 'WEEDY' or 'BEANSTALK' — when he chooses to talk to me.

Sometimes he calls me 'Stork, instead of 'Stalk'.

He also makes fun of me because he found out that I want to be like Lionel Messi.

On my locker, he crossed out my name and wrote 'MESSI', and then he crossed out 'MESSI' and wrote 'MESSY' next to it. He thinks that's funny. He should know that having to be so super neat is not my own choice and no reason for making fun of me.

... QUICKLY TURNING INTO THE WORST DAY EVER

Of cause, everyone wants to be Patrick's friend. What he says goes, not only on the soccer pitch.

His favorite trick is to trip me up, on and off the soccer pitch. I can never see it coming, and I fall over every time.

"Sorry, Spick, Ha, Ha, Ha! I couldn't see you. Oh, no! You've got dirt on you now! Ha, Ha!"

I try my best to think up ways to get back at Patrick and his friends, but my mind goes blank when I see them coming.

I usually don't like to take revenge for everything, but this is getting on my nerves big time.

Yesterday, Patrick bumped me with his elbow. I tripped and almost fell into the school pond. I just managed to keep upright and not fall in, but I had to step right into the weeds and slime at the edge of the pond.

He pretended to help me out, but instead, he pulled the blazer from my back and threw it into the middle of the pond. There it floated on top of the grime, sleeves outstretched and slowly spinning to the left.

"So sorry, ..." He grinned from ear to ear.

I pretended I didn't care. My shoes were full of pond water and dark green slime already. I waded in further to get my blazer back. I spun it around my head to shake the water out.

Pond water flew out to Patrick and his friends, covering them in grime.

"Sorry, I didn't see you from all the way here in the pond."

SQUELCH

SQUELCH

SLOSH

SLOSH

SLURP

Up the stairs and with each step up to math class, I left a trail of pond slime. There were green strands of algae and little leaves. I felt something moving in my shoe.

I put the blazer into my locker and took my shoe off. There was a small creature in it that I had never seen before, but I didn't want to show it to Mr. Mark because he would get mad at me.

When I sat down in class, I watched a small puddle forming under my chair. In fact, not only one puddle.

Of course, Mr. Mark was not impressed and gave me extra math homework to do.

Everyone was smirking behind their

hands, and the girls clamped their noses shut with their fingers:

"POOOOOOH, something stinks in here! It's nauseating!"

"Mr. Mark, I feel sick of the smell! Do something, PLEASE!"

I was mad — not just ordinary mad.

MAAAAAAAAD! MAD AS HELL!

I was shaking but not from being cold and wet.

I started to think about a plan. How could I make life miserable for Patrick, for once? But my mind was too mad to think clearly.

MY DIRT REBELLION PLAN

Instead of concentrating on math, I thought about what Mum would say. I could already hear her words in my head.

Eventually, I decided:

ENOUGH IS ENOUGH!

I HAVE TO do something to stop these things happening to me all the time.

I HAVE TO stand up for myself.

I want to be like everyone else — just normal.

I want everyone to respect me for who I am: MATT — THE FUTURE WORLD CUP SOCCER PLAYER.

I am done with everyone calling me

'Spick'

'Spotless'

'Match-Spick'

'Grime-less'

'Stork'.

And other names that I don't even want to think about.

I am done with being teased for my hairstyle.

I've had it because of my mirror-shiny shoes.

I AM FINISHED WITH THIS RUBBISH!

Mr. Mark asked me a question. I had no idea what he had said. His words had not even touched my ears, let alone my brain.

"What?"

"You need to pay attention, Matt. Concentrate! We have a math test next week."

Patrick smirked.

"Yeah, make sure you concentrate, Match-Spick, otherwise you may fall into a rabbit hole on your way home! Ha, Ha."

I ignored him. There are no rabbit holes on my way home or near my home anyway. My mind turned back to my problems.

WHY IS THIS HAPPENING TO ME?

How can I stop this all if I don't know the reasons for why people like teasing me?

I figured it all had to do with the way I look every day.

If Mum wouldn't be so obsessed with dirt, I wouldn't ALWAYS have to be so super extra clean and tidy every morning.

She packs all my things and lunch and snacks for me every morning to make sure I don't forget anything.

She even cuts the crusts off my sandwich and peels my mandarins for me.

If I weren't always so neat and clean and mollycoddled, I wouldn't be teased all the time.

If I had a different haircut, I would not be teased at all.

If I just could be a normal, average kid like everybody else, covered in ordinary dirt and grime! Life would be so much easier — and more fun too. And I probably would have more friends. Because — who would want to be friends with someone like me, the way I am now?

It dawned on me that I had to make a hard decision:

I HAVE TO stop Mum from treating me

like a baby.

If Mum wants to fight her war against dirt and germs — it's her war, not mine.

I don't want to fight a war AGAINST dirt and germs. I want to be a DIRT MAGNET until Mum realizes that a little bit of dirt won't hurt.

I want to be happy, so I can concentrate on becoming the world's best soccer player.

My decision was made.

If Patrick calls me 'Messy', that's what I will become.

I will become SUPER-MESSY.

Now, I only needed to work out a plan for getting it done. I decided to write my plan tonight.

MY DREAM OF BEING FILTHY DIRTY AND SUPER-MESSY

Mum picked me up from school, and I darted onto the back seat of her car, my blazer, feet, and shoes still soaked. I smelled like a pond bottom feeder. I was hoping she wouldn't notice, but she did.

SQUREECH. My shoes made a terrible noise in the back of the car. SLRRRPS. That was me on the backseat. SLAPP. That was my blazer.

All the way home she gave me a lecture about:

How she would need to get the car detailed because I made it all filthy.

How all the pond germs were now going to infest our house.

How I would get sick from being wet and cold.

How all the germs nesting in my skin would give me food poisoning.

How could it give me food poisoning? I

hadn't even drunk any of the pond water.

I started dreaming about what it would be like to be dirty.

Because — TOMORROW!

TOMORROW is going to be my first day of teaching Mum a thing or two about dirt and how it is now my best friend. I decided I would start strong and exaggerate my efforts of getting dirty.

I imagined the feeling of being dirty.

Really icky, sticky, yucky.

Filthy, grimy, grubby, and foul-smelling.

SOOOOO revolting and disgusting that everyone would want to vomit.

I want to be a DIRT MAGNET! I want to be MESSY all over! I want to spread MESS all around my life and the WHOLE WORLD!

Just for one day — or even just for half a day to start with.

Even a few minutes would be good.

My mind started to imagine how to find the dirtiest kind of dirt — and how to make it stick to me.

I then thought about how I could stick dirt onto things that belonged to others — like Isabelle's toothbrush, Patrick's lunch box, or Mum's kitchen towels — without them knowing that it was me who did it.

Soon my mind was filled with grimy ideas. I imagined how I would try and convince Mum that it would be better to leave a small amount of dirt on me than trying to fight her silly war on germs and dirt on my body.

Mum was talking all the way home.

"How could the school let this happen to

you? Who is responsible for looking after you when I am not there? The school, of course. But do they take their responsibility seriously? No. I will talk to them tomorrow and put a stop to this."

Great! Another reason for teasing me. Mum coming to school complaining of her little boy being infested with pond worms.

When we arrived home, Mum picked the clothes off my body and threw them into the washing machine. She washed my shoes out and dried them with kitchen paper.

"Disgusting!"

She made me have a shower.

"Make sure you get all this slime off your feet!"

"Yes, Mum."

A few more ideas came to me while I

was in the shower.

I put my first idea into action straight away:

I did not wash my hair with shampoo — just rinsed it with water. And I didn't wash my body with soap. It felt good. I am getting started, and that first step made me feel I was getting in control of my own life.

After dinner, I decided to write all my ideas down in a new notebook and make a test plan for each idea. On the front of the notebook, I wrote 'Math Problems'. I knew Mum would not look at a notebook with this title, and Isabelle did not care about math. Dad had never checked my things either, so this notebook was safe.

But first, I had to work out what type of dirt I would use and what I wouldn't use.

WHAT'S ALL THE FUSS ABOUT DIRT?

When I started writing my ideas down, I couldn't see what all the fuss was about dirt. I figured that most grownups think dirt is absolutely disgusting.

I totally don't agree with this. I don't think mud is disgusting at all. Snot can gross you out if it is someone else's snot that is landing on you, but it is just snot and not something that would make you die on the spot.

Same with poo. Everyone does it, the toilets at school have poo on it every day, and nobody dies from it. So, it can't be that bad. Dogs do it all over the park. When Grump does a whoopsie in the park, Dad just looks around to see if anyone is watching, and if not, he walks away and leaves the poo. The rain washes it away, and I think it makes the grass grow better.

Birds fly all over the place and poop on the grass or our washing line in full flight. Mum goes hyper about it and puts the washing straight back into the wash.

I figured that for grownups, dirt is mainly anything that sticks to kids and what they touch for longer than a second.

I decided to use just ordinary dirt, the type of everyday dirt that is all around every day, nothing super terrible like paint or car oil, or stuff that belongs to someone else for their work.

PART TWO

Here are my methods of becoming SUPER-MESSY, the dirt magnet. Some made a MEGA-mess, and some created just minor grubbiness that most parents and teachers wouldn't even notice.

I decided to test a new method every day to see how it could gross out everyone.

Especially in order of priority:

1. Mum,
2. Isabelle,
3. The kids and teachers at school,

4. Dad (who doesn't care much about dirt)
5. My friends (of which I don't have many, except Cameron, Dillon, and Owen next door).

I later found that I could create a mega-mess sometimes even without trying. These turned out to be the best ones.

CUTTING OFF THE PAST

"It's always good to follow through with your decisions."

That is what Dad always says. Most of the time, I hate it when he says that. But on this occasion, I thought it sounded good.

I wanted to start my journey to become messy with a BIG BANG. With this, I mean, I wanted to make a big change so that everyone could notice that I had changed overnight.

Why not change my hairstyle so that I don't look like this dude Elvis anymore?

After I had said goodnight to Mum and Dad and Isabelle, I waited until everyone had gone to bed and turned their lights out.

I tiptoed to the bathroom and locked myself in.

I had hidden the kitchen scissors under

my FC Barcelona top. Now I looked in the mirror and took them out. I held them against my head, this way and that to see where I should start cutting.

Carefully I grabbed the Elvis lock above my forehead and chopped it off in one swift cut.

Nice work! It looked a bit weird and unbalanced, I thought.

With a bit of effort, I managed to get the hair on top of my head cut quite evenly from side to side. It looked a bit like a dinosaur back with ridges.

I tried to cut a new fringe like Lionel Messi's fringe, but unfortunately, I slipped a bit with the scissors. That made a big hole into my fringe. I tried to improve it, but in the end, I had cut out a big triangle of hair above my left eye.

Nothing I could do about that now. What's done is done.

I debated with myself in my mind whether I should take another triangle out above my right eye, but I decided against it.

I found it hard to cut the hair at the back of my head. When I tried to look at it in the mirror, it seemed quite patchy.

Overall, I was satisfied.

No way anyone couldn't notice that I had changed.

I gathered up the hair on the floor and threw it in the toilet. Unfortunately, most of it wouldn't flush down. I went to bed, looking forward to the reaction of Mum and Dad the next morning.

Results? Excellent and predictable.

When I sat down for breakfast, Mum took one look at me and dropped her plate:

"EEEEEEEK! What have you DONE?"

Dad groaned.

"That looks hideous. But it's your head. You have to walk around like that today, not me." He shook his head and poured himself another cup of coffee.

You should have heard Mum all the way to school.

"What is grandma going to say? The hairdresser can't fix this. He is going to shave your head! You had such nice hair. Now it is all ruined!"

I didn't care. In fact, I was extremely happy with the results of my efforts.

The kids at school shrieked and rolled on the floor, laughing their heads off. Mr. Mark put on a very crooked smirk but didn't say anything. Everyone snickered when they looked at me, but NOBODY called me 'Spick' all day.

Patrick called me 'Tee Rex'.

After school, Mum took me to the hairdresser. He tried to do his best to make a hairstyle out of my 'hair disaster' as Mum called it. In the end, I still had a fringe of some kind, not very different from Lionel Messi's. The back and sides of my head were shaved to get rid of the bare patches, and the dinosaur ridges were evened out a bit.

Not bad. I now looked quite normal, almost like Lionel Messi.

Dad gave me the thumbs up when he came home.

For the rest of the day, I kept out of Mum's way as much as I could. I went to bed, satisfied that my day had turned out better than expected.

THE TOOTHBRUSH TRICKERY

Ov
ernight, I had prepared myself for trying
the next messiness trick in the morning.

Mum always makes us brush our teeth after breakfast and dinner, so our teeth won't "rot out" as she calls it. It is very irritating because she doesn't know that we keep eating our hidden sweets in bed after brushing our teeth.

With this trick, I wanted to show Mum that I was going to start turning the world into a messy place. Maybe she would start thinking that a little bit of dirt in the bathroom is not a big deal.

I made sure I was the last one in the bathroom to brush my teeth before leaving for school.

I shut the bathroom door and took my toothbrush out of the holder. I put some toothpaste and water on it and rubbed the toothpaste thoroughly into the bristles until they looked white and slimy.

I then pointed the bristles to the mirror and dragged my fingers over them to make the slime splutter onto the mirror and sink. I achieved quite an even splatter, very creative. I also got some on my face.

I thought it did not look quite slimy and disgusting enough, though. How could I improve it?

I spread a bit of soap and water on my hands to create bubbly slime. I wiped my hands on the mirror and pretended I was trying to clean the mirror. Of course, it made a bigger mess than with just the toothpaste dots.

I was happy with the result. Good!

"Come on! It's time to leave! Dad is waiting!"

Dad tooted the horn outside.

I darted out of the bathroom, grabbed my bag, and rushed into Dad's car.

I had not brushed my teeth.

SPAGHETTI ODDITY

I sat behind Dad on our way to school, dreaming out the window.

I need to get better with my messiness. I need to be messier.

Then I had an idea.

Mum wants me to wash my hands all the time: Before eating, after eating, after toilet, after school, after soccer training, after touching the dog. You name it; everything is a reason for her to make me wash my hands. She says it stops germs growing on me.

I decided I would not wash my hands at all today.

For fruit snack, Mum had packed some orange wedges. Instead of just sucking out the juice, I picked the pips out with my fingers and flicked them at Patrick. Then I slurped the juice out of the wedges. It was a satisfying feeling when I wiped my mouth on my sleeves and my hands on my pants. Fortunately, my hands were still all sticky afterward.

At lunch break, I ate my leftover Spaghetti Bolognaise from yesterday's dinner with my fingers instead of using the fork that Mum had packed for me.

SLURP, SLURP.

The spaghetti slithered into my mouth, splattering tomato sauce on my collar and my face. Some of it ended up on the girls sitting next to me. They were disgusted.

"AAARRR"

"YUCK"

"REEEEVOLTING!"

The boys rolled their eyes.

Spaghetti was also on special at the canteen and Robbie copied me. He tried to be even more outrageous by throwing the spaghetti into the air to catch them with his mouth.

Great trick, but it didn't work for me.

I tried to catch mine with the fork out of the air. That did not work either.

Jacob had grabbed his spaghetti from the canteen and dropped it on his head, I could hear him muttering the words *"Oh look! I'm Matt, and my Elvis hair has grown back."*

We managed to have more food on the floor than in our mouths.

My hands were even stickier now.

After lunch, we had science. We went outside to work in teams to find insects and other living creatures in our school garden. I decided to dig for worms.

I used my fingers to dig holes in the lettuce garden bed, but I couldn't find a single worm. I inspected my hands and found they had taken on a nice dark brown color. Rubbing them together made my hands less sticky than before, but the color stayed on.

I did not wash my hands all day at school.

Not washing hands is an excellent method to get used to being grubby. If grownups wipe their hands after touching your fingers, you know you had a successful day.

Unfortunately, Mum made me wash my hands when I got home and again before dinner. I had not managed a whole day without washing my hands, but it was a good start.

I saw that Mum had cleaned the bathroom mirror and sink. It was spotless again. She didn't say anything to me. Maybe she thought that it was Dad who had messed it up.

FOLLOWING MESSI'S MUDDY FOOTSTEPS

Today turned out to become the messiest day so far after I had decided to become a dirt magnet.

Because it was Saturday morning, we played our weekly school soccer game, and I scored a goal. Almost from the corner with a left-footer into the top back corner of the goal. The goalkeeper of the B-team, Patrick, never had a chance. He had run out towards me, but I got the ball past him.

Everyone admired my new hairstyle

"Great hairstyle you have now, Matt!"

"You look like a real human being now, Matt!"

"I would have shaved all of it off."

These were some of the comments I got about how I looked now.

It had started raining, and by the end of the game, we were all as wet and muddy as drowned rats. My soccer uniform had green blotches all over from the grass, and my legs were covered in brown mud from top to bottom. You couldn't even see the color of my soccer boots anymore because of the clods of mud on them.

I loved it.

Mum hates mud. Full stop. Mud of any kind. Anywhere. On anything, especially me and my clothes.

Dad patted me on the back after the game.

"Well done! That goal was spectacular, FIFA style! Lionel Messi couldn't have done it better!"

On the way home, he stopped at Maccas and let me have chips and a burger.

When we got home, Mum made me take off my soccer gear and have a shower.

Then we had lunch — tomato soup. I tried to slurp as loud as possible.

"Manners!" Isabelle and Mum said with one   voice.

MUDLYMPICS

After lunch, I went over to Owen's house.

My one and only friend outside of

school, besides Grump, is Owen. He lives next door and is also in the Golden Square District Soccer Club. His garden is much bigger than ours and has a gate to the park.

We played a bit of FIFA 18 and then we went outside.

Owen has a bike, and he lent me his mother's bike so that we could go for a ride in the park.

It had stopped raining, but there were still lots of puddles in the park, both on the walking tracks and on the grass.

We found an excellent puddle where the path stopped, just before the BMX track.

First, we tested it out, driving through it slowly. The puddle turned out to be quite long and wide and not very deep.

We raced through it, and then we started from opposite ends, racing into the puddle, one from each end and passing each other right in the middle of it.

The water sprayed right up to our waists.

Then we tried a new trick. Racing as fast as possible into the middle of the puddle and then doing a sliding stop.

YOOHOO!

SPLASH

SCREECH

SPLATTER.

My bicycle slipped out from under me, and I landed in the puddle.

Owen tried it next to see if he could slide his bike on its side too.

He slid even further than me.

YAY!

The sliding stops stirred up a lot of mud in the puddle.

We then tried to create even more murkiness by doing a sliding stop and spinning the bike on the spot at the same time.

After a while, we looked at each other and started laughing.

Owen had black mud spots all over his face, his hair, and his clothes, even on his back.

"You look like you have mud measles!"

"You too, your Mum will have a fit when she sees you!

"Doesn't matter. I want to make the most of this mud. I am a MUD MAGNET. Yoo-hoo! Let's take a few more rounds through this puddle!"

Off we went again, and the puddle got deeper and deeper and muddier and muddier, the mud slimier and slimier.

Our bikes were covered in it, but we were happy.

I think we got much better at sliding stops. We had perfected this skill.

"Maybe tomorrow, we could get Dillon over with his bike too and do it again".

Owen nodded.

"Cameron also has a bike, and he is really good at jumping with it on the BMX track".

We went back to Owen's garden and hosed the bikes down with the garden hose. They looked as good as new, even cleaner than when we started.

I was a bit worried about what Owen's Mum would say when she saw us two mudlarks.

HOW OWEN'S MUM DEALS WITH MUD

Owen's Mum came to the door and gave us a long look:

"O. M. G. Now I have to hose you off!"

She had watched us through the window.

I kicked off my runners. They were full of muddy water.

Owen tipped mud out of his gumboots.

"OH NO, my poor gumboots!" Owen's Mum was not exactly happy. He had used his Mum's gumboots instead of his own.

"They will dry again, Mum!"

"Sure, Owen! In two weeks, maybe? What am I going to wear when I take Patch for a walk? Your runners?". Patch is Owen's dog. He is tiny and white with a brown eye patch.

Owen's brother David pretends that Patch is his dog. Here is a picture of Owen, David, and Patch.

Owen's Mum put the shower on and told us to rinse the mud off.

We climbed in the shower and rinsed most of the mud down the plughole before we peeled our socks and clothes off and dropped them on the floor.

After that, Owen's Mum let us have a bubble bath. I borrowed some of Owen's clothes even though they were far too short for me, and after that, Owen's Mum gave us hot chocolate.

We played a bit more FIFA 18, and then it was time to go home for dinner.

Owen's Mum had hosed our clothes down some more in the garden and put Owen's in the washing machine. Mine were in a plastic bag to take home to Mum.

I put the plastic bag next to the washing machine.

"Hi, Mum, Owen and I had a great time!"

"Where are your clothes? What happened?"

"Nothing much, they just got a little bit muddy."

"WHAAAT?"

Mum jumped up, and her scream in the laundry was spectacular.

I was completely happy — and I hadn't even been trying very hard to get dirty.

On a scale of 1 to 10, this had been a 10-point   day.

ALWAYS BE PREPARED!

It had rained some more overnight but not enough to cancel Sunday's Golden Square District Soccer match.

Dad drove me, Owen, and his little brother David to the Mill Post Soccer field where our game was. We looked like sparkly sunflowers on the green grass in our gold-colored uniforms.

We tried hard, but we lost 17–Nil. Our goalie is too small, I think. I almost got a goal in, but I just missed.

After the match, Dad dropped Owen and David off at their door and parked the car in the garage.

Mum didn't say anything about my muddy uniform this time. Maybe she is learning by now and realizes that mud is becoming part of my life. Perhaps she will get used to it — eventually.

She had made pancakes for us. Maple syrup is great for getting it to stick to you and everything else. It is see-through and not visible when it is on your hands. I poured a bit of it on my hands and rubbed it in my hair.

I felt I needed to do something disgusting to show that I had liked the pancakes. I gathered up all the strength in my belly and pushed out a humongous burp, a big bubble of gas from the depth of my stomach right out over the table.

Dad looked at me but said nothing.

Mum's eyes grew as big as saucers.

"MATT! That is totally unacceptable!"

Isabelle rolled her eyes:

"You're disgusting, you filthy worm!"

"No need to call me names!" I protested.

"Clear the table!" Mum ordered. "That will give you something useful to do."

Dad stood up and did a big stretch.

"I am going to have a rest now." He says that every Sunday after lunch, but I know he just wants to watch soccer on TV in the bedroom.

Mum said she was going to visit the flower show with her best friend in the afternoon.

"Isabelle, you and Dad can look after Matt while I am not here. Make sure he doesn't get into trouble."

"Yes, Mum." Isabelle glared at me and went off to her room, leaving her door open.

I promised I would be nice and quiet and not make any noise.

"Dad, can I take Grump for a walk later?"

"Sounds like a great idea, but make sure he doesn't' t get dirty."

"Of course!"

Dad closed his bedroom door. I knew he

wouldn't come out until Mum was home in the evening.

I played FIFA 18 for a little while, but then I thought I should take Grump for a walk.

I listened — no sound from Mum and Dad's bedroom. Isabelle was on the phone with her best friend.

I thought about how much fun we had yesterday in the mud. What could I do today to prove that I am now a professional dirt magnet?

I clipped the leash to Grump's collar and went out through the laundry door, careful to not make a noise.

READY — SET — MUD

I knocked on Owen's door and asked whether he wanted to go for a walk in the park with Grump and Patch.

Owen was right for it but said we had to

take David with us because his Mum and Dad were having a snooze after lunch.

We let Grump loose in Owen's garden so he could have some fun with Patch first while we were thinking about what to do in the park.

Eventually, we came up with an idea.

Mum and Dad like Grump to be clean. When Dad takes Grump for a walk, he doesn't go far into the park with him. He lets him run around for a bit while he stands there looking at his mobile phone, checking emails, and the news.

He doesn't usually care what Grump does. When it rains, and Grump has dirty feet, Dad just dries them off at home with a towel and wipes the floor clean afterward.

When I was younger, I taught Grump to fetch sticks and tennis balls and bring them back to me. Now, I can throw a ball anywhere, and Grump will run after it. I even use one of my old soccer balls and kick it as far away as possible for Grump to fetch.

We found a bucket and one of Owen's old soccer balls. Patch had already destroyed some of the ball, and bits of the outer layer were hanging off it. Patch carried the ball, grabbing it with his teeth. He could barely lift it. It was still good enough for what we wanted to do today.

David jumped up and down in anticipation, just like Patch.

"What do we do with the bucket?"

"You'll see. Just be patient!"

That's very hard for David. Patience is not one of his strengths.

We went into the park and straight to

yesterday's puddle. It had become even bigger and deeper. Black and ominous.

Owen took a stick and started stirring. The dogs were watching and sniffing, wondering what we were looking for in the puddle.

"David, we need to make mud balls."

"How big?"

"Just so that you can throw them. Not too big. Look, like this."

Owen made a ball as big as a donut and rolled it in his hands.

"Just make sure there are no stones or sticks in it."

David started fishing in the mud soup, and we all started rolling mud balls. We gently placed them into the bucket.

"Now, let's throw a ball into the puddle and see if the dogs will go and fetch it."

I held Grump by the collar with one hand, and David held Patch.

Owen threw a mud ball into the puddle.

SPLASH

"Let Patch go!"

David let go, but Patch just kept sitting and looking at Owen.

"Go fetch!"

Patch didn't move.

"Let me try with Grump!"

I took a ball out of the bucket and showed it to Grump. I raised my hand, making sure that Grump was watching the mud ball.

Then I let it go right into the middle of the puddle.

SPLASH

Grump was off like a dart, racing after the ball. He jumped into the puddle, with Patch running after him.

Grump was pawing the puddle trying to find the ball, but that had turned back into mud again.

We played this game for a while, but in the end, Grump thought it was a bad game and didn't want to run after the mud balls anymore.

We changed to the old soccer ball, and we all had a great time with it. I used my soccer skills to kick the ball right into the middle of the puddle so that the dogs had to jump right into it to get the ball.

Because the ball didn't bounce anymore, it made a gigantic thud hitting the puddle.

THUD.

SPLASH.

THUD.

SPLASH.

The dogs were happy and didn't mind getting wet.

David wanted to outdo the dogs and raced with them in and out of the mud.

He had the idea to have a mud ball fight.

THUD.

PLOP.

WOOSH.

SLURP.

After a while, we got tired of it, and David and Patch were cold.

We went back to Owen's garden and hosed the dogs down with the garden hose. They were not happy about it, but they were a little bit less muddy after that. We let them shake most of the water off, and then we toweled them down in Owen's laundry.

What now?

While Owen and I were busy with the dogs, David jumped up and down and made mud handprints all over the glass door of Owen's house. We could have left them there, but we thought we better hose the doors too.

Owen said that we should get cleaned up in our house because it was his Mum's turn yesterday. I agreed.

"But I don't want Patch to come over too."

It was bad enough to have David with us because he is always so noisy. And I didn't want to get Dad and Isabelle's attention.

We let Patch into Owen's house and

turned the heater on so that he could get warm.

"David, you can come with us. But you must be quiet as a mouse. If you make any noise, I will throw your soccer ball into the trash when we get home."

We tiptoed out of Owen's garden door and   over   to   our   house.

CLEANUP DIRT MAGNET STYLE

Just like the day before, all our clothes were mega-wet and muddy. They were in a complete state of filth and sliminess.

Our shoes were like lifeboats that someone had recovered from a stranded shipwreck. Our hair and faces were caked in mud. My hair still had maple syrup in it and was like a mud crust helmet.

Brilliant and very satisfying.

It had taken us a bit of effort yesterday to get the mud off our bodies, and Owen's Mum had done the trick with her washing machine to get our clothes back into a civilized state.

What would we do today?

We gently opened our front door. I kept holding Grump by the lead and, at the same time, tried to hop from one foot to the other to get my shoes off.

Owen tried to make Yeti footprints by spinning around on the spot. That got some mud on the hallway walls.

We tossed our shoes out of the way and sloshed into the bathroom in our socks. We made long dark streaks on the hallway floor.

I shut the bathroom door. It was a bit crowded with Owen, David, me and Grump.

What next?

We decided to have a bath because we were cold now. David's teeth were chattering.

"Be quiet, David!". David tried to chatter his teeth with less noise.

We tipped half a bottle of shampoo into the bathwater to make a mountain of bubbles. Some of it flowed over onto the floor.

Grump sat next to the bathtub, watching us.

When the water got cold, we got out and dried ourselves off. We piled the towels together with our muddy clothes into a heap on the bathroom floor. I tiptoed to my bedroom to get clean, dry ones from my room for all of us.

Isabelle was still on her phone, and I heard no noise from Dad's bedroom. He had probably fallen asleep. Good.

We got dressed, ready to go into the living room.

Grump had a glorious wet dog smell on him, but he was still very damp because of his thick fur. And he still had mud balls between his toes.

We took a new towel to dry him a bit more.

After that, Grump was happy to bounce right onto the carpet next to the heater.

I got him a sofa cushion to rest his head on it.

We put FIFA 18 on, and Owen and I started playing.

David was bored.

"SSSHHH, David, be quiet! Otherwise, you need to go home. Here, have some biscuits."

I gave him my mobile phone, and that kept him quiet for a while with playing games.

We had wrapped him in a blanket to warm him up.

After a while, we heard Mum opening the front door.

"Darling, I am home! YIKES!! WHAT HAS HAPPENED HERE?"

She must have seen the mud on the hallway walls and floor. We had forgotten to wipe it off.

But then I thought that this was all part of my plan to turn my life into a gigantic mess.

Mum came into the living room, her face red like a tomato.

"Can we have some food, please? We are so hungry!"

Mum had an absolute hissy-fit when she looked at Grump and us.

"You have done it AGAIN! Why do you have to get covered in mud all the time? That is DISGUSTING!"

"ISABELLE! Is that how you look after your brother when I am not here?"

Owen got up. He grabbed David's hand and pulled him off the sofa.

"I think we better go now."

They were out like a flash.

"Isabelle, you can clean up this mess now, you did not pay attention to what I said. It's your fault that this house is in such a state now. So, go and fix it."

Isabelle waved her fist at me but said nothing.

She cleaned up the mess and put all the clothes into the washing machine. I thought the mud would probably grind the motor to a stop.

It had been a very successful day today, full of mud and mess.

I was happy. Grump was happy too. Best of all, Isabelle was very unhappy because she had to TOUCH mud.

All in all — a very good day.

When I went to bed, I found that Isabelle had put my wet and muddy runners into my pillow cover. My pillow had turned all muddy.

"What goes around comes around, little brother. You are not so smart, after all."

I had to get a new pillow cover and a towel to cover the wet pillow.

Thanks, Isabelle. Who is the inventor of messiness here, me or you? But not a bad idea, I thought, I might try it on someone else in the future.

But now I had to think about what I would do for tomorrow, Monday.

THE GREAT SLIME ESCAPE

In the morning, Mum watched me like a hawk, so I could not do anything to spoil the 'immaculate' look of my school uniform and my appearance. She had made me have a shower and asked me to keep the bathroom door open. She kept watching what I did, and therefore, I could not make another mess in there without her knowing.

At school, everyone looked at me closely to see if I had made any other changes to my appearance over the weekend.

"Hey, Matt, what's up?"

Cameron came up to me. "Do you want to play soccer at recess?"

"Sure."

Cameron is my best friend at school. He is also very good at soccer, and he wants to be like Cristiano Ronaldo. I don't let him know that I think Lionel Messi is better than Cristiano Ronaldo. He might get upset and stop being my friend.

Every Monday after lunch we have Enviro-Science, and this time Mr. Mark asked us to find and write down all the creatures we could see after all the rain over the weekend.

On my list were:

Birds: 6 different species.

Mammals: 1 Koala.

Frogs: 2 different species under the big leaves of the rhubarb plants and near the pond.

Snails: One kind of snail with a house on top, also near the rhubarb.

Slugs: Two kinds, one brown and small, one big and more orange.

Slaters: One kind, under a piece of rotten wood and under a rock.

That gave me an idea. I hurried back to my locker to get my lunchbox, and then I went on to gather all the slugs I could find into the lunchbox.

It was easy because there were so many of them.

When my lunchbox was half full, I added a few pieces of grass and rhubarb leaves and shut the box.

The good thing with slugs is that they are slimy, and when you touch them, they make even more slime to gross you out. They think you then won't want to eat them. But I don't really know what slugs think with their small brains. Maybe, they don't think at all.

I shut the lunchbox and put it back into my backpack in the locker.

My hands were slimy from the slugs, and the slime didn't come off even when I tried to rub it off on my pants. I thought it was a good type of slime for grossing out everyone.

"Look, isn't this slime magnificent?"

I waved my hands in front of Jacob's face.

"AAAAAAR!"

I pushed my fingers right up to Larissa's eyes.

"YUUUUCK!"

"Hey Patrick, would you like a taste of this?"

"Don't touch me!"

I smiled to myself in my mind. Great success!

After the last bell, we had soccer practice, and we got muddy again.

Dad picked me up because Mum had

taken Isabelle to dance practice.

At home, I took out the lunchbox and went to the garage to get Isabelle's old birdcage. She once had a blue budgerigar, but Mum didn't like the dust it made, and so Isabelle had to give up her budgie.

I dusted off the cage and put a piece of cardboard in its bottom drawer. When I tipped all the slugs on the cardboard, they just sat there in a heap and didn't wriggle much. I softly shut the cage door and went inside to place the cage on top of Isabelle's desk. Hopefully, she would gross out from the slimy creatures in her birdcage.

I gently shut her bedroom door so she wouldn't notice straight away that I had been in her room.

Dad made dinner that evening, and when Mum and Isabelle came home, we sat down to eat straight away.

"I am so happy with Isabelle's dancing; she is making great progress now.".

Mum was in a good mood. She hadn't noticed that I still had mud on my hands and suspicious grey marks all over my arms. That was where the slugs had stuck to my skin and left their slime.

"Take the plates out and put them in the dishwasher, kids, and then it's shower time and off to bed. It's late now.

Another shower! Not again.

I went into my room looking for my FC Barcelona top when I heard a blood-curdling shriek from Isabelle's bedroom.

"AAAAAAAARRRRR!"

"EEEEEEEEEEH!"

"NOOOOOOOOOOOOO!"

We all raced to Isabelle's room. Here she was, standing in the middle of the carpet, pointing to her desk.

There, on the top of the desk and mousepad, on the walls above the desk and on her chair, was my army of slugs, slithering off in all different directions. Some slowly, some faster, and some were just sitting there. Only a few were still in the cage. I hadn't anticipated that the slugs would escape through the gaps between the bars of the cage.

That was even better.

"That's for putting muddy shoes in my pillow yesterday."

Isabelle started crying.

"I am not taking them off! They are SOOOOO disgusting!"

I grinned.

"I am happy to do it for you."

I got a jar out of the pantry and picked

up every slug that I could find. I showed Isabelle how they stuck to my hands and how gross their slime was. She shrieked a bit more until Dad said I should stop it now.

I may not have found all the slugs, but most of them ended up in the jar. I took them to the backdoor and let them loose on the lawn with the lid open, so they could get something to eat.

Then I had my shower.

I had finally become a magnet of slime and messiness. The more I tried to wash off the slug slime, the slimier it got. It spread all over my arms, and I couldn't get it off.

Never mind, I thought, this is what I wanted. I had now become a successful dirt and slime magnet. Maybe I could keep it on until school tomorrow.

Mum came in to inspect me.

"This is revolting, get it off at once!"

That was easier said than done. This stuff had a way of sticking to me and not coming off. I gave up and accepted that I had to live with a slime cover for now.

I got out of the shower and dried myself off. The dry towel took some of the slime off, and Mum attacked the rest of it afterward with vinegar and paper towels.

Now I stank like vinegar on top of still being slimy in patches.

I went to bed, satisfied, and wondering what I would do tomorrow.

SAY AHHHHHH — GRRRRRRRR

At school, I didn't have an opportunity to look for more dirt. We had a big math test and then music and reading. I didn't eat my lunch sandwich because Mum had again cut all the crusts off. She must think I am still in Kindergarten.

I kept thinking about what I would do today to make the world a messier place, but I didn't come up with any new ideas.

After lunch, Mr. Mark sent Patrick and me out to check whether the school chicken had laid any eggs. Amy and Nicola came with us to check on the chickens' feed and water.

Oh, No! Patrick and I on the same team!

I started to get worried. Surely, Patrick would come up with something to torment me.

Off we went, and sure enough, there were six eggs in the chicken coop laying boxes.

Patrick held the egg carton, and I bent down to carefully scoop up each egg.

One, two, three, four.

BANG

Yellow goo ran down my face. I got such a shock that I accidentally crushed the fifth egg in my hand

Patrick had smashed one of the eggs on my head.

"I think you need some styling product on your hair! Ha, Ha, Ha! Now you look REALLY messy!"

I scooped up the sixth egg and threw it at him. He must have expected that and just ducked. The egg flew past him and ended up on Amy's jumper.

That wasn't meant to happen! I like Amy.

"Sorry, Amy, it was meant to hit Patrick!"

She looked at me with fire in her eyes and ran off to the washroom.

I just wiped the eggshells off my head and rubbed the gooey egg stuff through my hair. It would dry just fine. At least, Patrick had found a way to make me messier.

"Thanks, Patrick, I will look great with this hairstyle."

When we got back to class, Mr. Mark gave us both extra homework to do.

"Because you are so interested in the inner workings of eggs, you will write a 200-word assignment, due tomorrow, on the value of eggs."

I think I will ask Mum about how much she pays for a carton of eggs, and then I will debate whether that is too much or a fair price.

I kept thinking about what I would do at home today. Then I had an idea.

If you have a sister like mine, you can

bet that she will be very fussy about her appearance. Isabelle calls it 'particular'.

"I am very particular about the way I look."

Isabelle torments me every day about the way I look and the way I behave, and she tells her friends that I am the worst brother that any girl can have. She never thinks that she is the most annoying sister a boy can have.

As I mentioned before, I had an idea about how to keep Grump's teeth healthy. You guessed it. Today was the day I was going to give it a go.

The idea involved Isabelle's toothbrush and toothpaste to brush Grump's teeth.

I took Grump to the bathroom and shut the door. I put toothpaste on Isabelle's pink brush and rubbed it into the bristles.

I then leaned over Grump's back and held his mouth with one hand, forcing the toothbrush between his lips. He shook his head, and the toothbrush fell out of my hand.

"No, Grump. Sit!"

Grump sat down — what a good dog.

Unfortunately, Grump was not very cooperative and kept spitting Isabelle's toothbrush out. I tried to wrestle with him, but in the end, he bit the toothbrush in half and spat out the pieces.

Maybe he didn't like the taste of Isabelle's toothbrush, or he didn't like the taste of the toothpaste.

If you have a cooperative dog, you can try this, but don't hold your breath about it being successful.

I think this experiment was the only failure so far in my plan to make

Isabelle's world a messier place.

I wouldn't recommend this as some dogs might bite. But I would definitely recommend telling your annoying sister that you will try this soon. It will be enough for her to hide her toothbrush from   you.

TWO WEEKS OF GUNK

It had stopped raining for a while now, and I couldn't find any more mud to get messy with. The puddles in the park had dried up, and the soccer pitches were getting firmer.

That is why I concentrated on finding new methods of keeping the dirt on me that had somehow stuck to me. My goal was to stay messy as long as possible after some grime or dirt had attached itself to my body.

My routine went something like this now:

In the morning before school, I would not allow Mum to brush my hair anymore. The harder she tried, the more I shook my head to escape her hairbrush.

"I am old enough to brush my own hair!"

"You will get lice in your hair if you don't brush it."

"No, I won't."

After a few days, Mum gave up on my hair.

Success.

Some days I also did not brush my teeth. I didn't like the feeling of fur on my teeth, but I thought I needed to suffer that feeling to be a true dirt magnet.

At night, I tried to avoid soap at all costs. I used several methods of keeping soap and shampoo from touching my body. Obviously, Mum would soon catch on to that I didn't have a shower if she found dry towels in the bathroom.

I also had to pretend that I had washed my hair.

My first method was to turn on the shower and let it run for a while. Then I would drip some shampoo on the shower floor, and then I would throw the towel into the shower to get it wet. After that, I would take it out and pretend to dry myself with it. It would wet my hair just enough for passing as washed.

My second method was to hold my head under the shower sideways and dry it with my towel.

Both methods worked well.

Some days I would put a bit of shampoo on my head, so it smelt like I washed my hair.

I avoided washing my ears, my feet, and my armpits.

All the dirt after soccer practice and games was just ordinary dirt that came off quickly without soap, by standing under the shower.

Nobody at home or school seemed to notice that I had not used much soap for a week.

After about two weeks of this, Patrick stared at me, his face screwed up.

"You got wax in your ears, Dirt Ball!"

The whole class burst into laughter.

"Really? How did it get there?"

"Dunno, maybe it grows in your ears, Ha, Ha, Ha!"

Finally, I had started to be as revolting as I could possibly be.

I HAD GROSSED OUT PATRICK!

It hadn't even been hard to get to this point.

The kids at school had stopped calling me Spick for a while, but I found that most of them had started avoiding me.

That is not what I had expected.

I decided to keep going with being messy, and during the next week, I also did not cut my fingernails and toenails. My long toenails made holes in my socks, so I had to cut them eventually because they hurt when I was wearing my soccer boots.

I decided that soccer comes first and being messy second.

SNOT ROCKET

I kept going with my goal of avoiding soap for a couple more weeks, but then I got sick. Dillon had come to school, sick with a cold. He passed it on to most of us, especially to his friends like Cameron and me.

Mum said it was my fault because I had turned into a complete feral slime ball over the last three weeks. She said that this was the reason why germs had attacked me and that I now had to suffer the consequences.

I felt miserable, and my head hurt. My nose was dripping, and my ears were blocked. I kept sneezing all the time. Mum wanted to keep me at home, but I said I wanted to go to school. It was just too boring at home.

I worked out that I could do a lot with snot to gross out Mum and Isabelle at home and the kids at school.

Firstly, I did not wipe my nose with tissues. I wiped my nose on my shoulders and sleeves and achieved beautiful snot streaks on my school jumper.

Mr. Mark had told us to sneeze into our elbows if we had to sneeze. That would help stop the germs from flying onto other people.

I thought that it was all too late for that as most of us were snotty already. We all kept sneezing as loudly as possible, right into the air in front of us. During recess, we measured how far we could sneeze our snot. Patrick won, as usual.

The girls did not like this game and told us we belonged in the Zoo.

At home, Mum gave me a box of tissues to use. I just wiped my nose and then dropped the tissues on the floor. Grump picked them up and pulled them apart with his teeth. He probably was looking for something to eat in them.

Mum was in despair.

"GRRRRR! You two are a challenge!"

Yes! I like being a challenge.

By the end of the week, I was much better. I had stopped sneezing.

Mum had become stricter with me about being clean. She had also discovered my ear wax. Of course, she had to take me to the doctor to get my ears washed out with a syringe. That was a revolting experience that I cannot recommend to anyone.

It hadn't been a fun week, but I was sure next week would be full of new dirt fun.

SAUSAGE PAINTING

For the next few weeks, I battled with Mum in a tug of war of minds. She tried her best to get me clean and keep me clean, and I tried my best to get dirty and stay dirty. Every time she discovered and complained about a speck of dirt on me, I said in a quiet and friendly little voice:

"A little bit of dirt won't hurt!"

Every time I said that she rolled her eyes.

"Yes, Yes, I know, but not on you."

I asked whether I could invite Cameron and Owen over for a sleepover on Saturday.

"If you promise not to make a complete mess of yourselves and the house, you can invite them."

"I promise. Pinkie promise!"

On Saturday, Dad picked Cameron and me up from the school soccer game and drove us home. Owen came over when he saw our car pulling up outside our house.

Mum said she would make sausages for lunch while we could go out to the park for a little while.

We took Grump, Patch, and our soccer balls and practiced our soccer skills, mainly passing and dribbling.

When Dad called us inside, we sat down at the table straight away.

Mum had forgotten to ask us to wash our hands.

She put a pile of sausages in front of us, as well as bread rolls, butter, and a bottle each of ketchup, barbeque sauce, and mustard.

We were starving and poured ketchup all over our plates to dip the sausages in.

Nobody talked until we had all finished three sausages each. Then Cameron reached for another sausage.

I took the ketchup bottle and pointed it towards his plate.

"Whoopsie, I didn't mean to do that."

The ketchup hadn't landed on his plate but his arm.

"Nice try! Here you go!"

He took the mustard bottle and pointed it at my face. With a gigantic squeeze, he shot a large splotch of mustard under my left eye.

PLOP

"This looks like a snot launcher. Or a snot rocket."

"Yes, and this looks like a blood bath." Owen ripped the ketchup bottle out of my hand and squeezed catchup over Cameron's head. The bottle was almost empty now.

I took the barbeque sauce bottle and pointed it at Owen.

"And this looks like runny poo!"

We could not stop laughing. Owen dipped his sausage onto the ketchup on Cameron's head and then used it to spread the mustard on my face.

"You look like an oil painting now! Ha, Ha!"

Mum came over from the kitchen to see what was so funny. She glared at me. Obviously, this was all my fault.

"You don't seem to be hungry anymore! Go and wash this disgusting mess off yourselves."

We went to the bathroom, and Owen held Cameron's head under the tap to wash the ketchup off. I just wiped my face off with a towel. Owen did the same.

It had been great fun, but we decided to not push our luck too much for the rest of the day.

There   was   always   tomorrow.

THE STINK BUS

I found it hard to think of new ways of getting myself messy or creating a mess for others.

But luckily, Mr. Mark organized a farm visit to our district community farm. The idea was to show us where our food comes from.

YAY! WE ARE GOING ON A BUS!

I was running to the backseat with Cameron and Dillon. We were hoping that we would be far enough away from Mr. Mark and Patrick's mum, to start some mischief at the back of the bus.

Patrick's mum always comes to our school excursions as an 'extra pair of hands'. That's what she calls it, but I think she just wants to be a stickybeak to see what her little boy learns.

The journey started in quite a harmless way on the main road, but as we went deeper into the countryside, the roads had lots of bends. We were thrown about in the back of the bus.

We tried to hold on to the seats in front

of us, but it still did not stop us from swaying left and right.

After a few more bends in the road, Dillon's face became all crumpled up.

"I feel sick!"

He bent over and spewed his breakfast all over himself and the floor.

"Ooaarr, Ooor, Aaaarwwash!"

It stank all sour and disgusting. I looked at the mess and thought it was quite creative in color. But, just looking at it made me sick too, and I had to vomit right next to Dillon's breakfast. I wiped my face with my sleeves. Now that my food was out, I felt better.

Patrick's mum got up and came to the back of the bus.

"You poor things! Never mind. Here are tissues and a rubbish bag. Wipe it off and put it all in the bag. We will be there soon so you can wash this stuff off."

The stink in the bus made a couple more of the kids throw up too.

When we arrived, all the vomiters had to go the bathrooms first to clean themselves up, and then we went through the turnstiles to meet the animals.

PAT-LYMPICS

First off, the farm manager took us to
meet the goats. There were three goats,
a fat one, a medium one, and a small
one. The one I was most afraid of was
the fat one because it was the only one

with horns, and by the look of its mouth, I don't think Mum would have called it 'immaculate'.

Mum had made me a jam sandwich for lunch.

I think the fat goat could smell the jam sandwich because it came up to me and snatched it right out of my school bag, paper bag and all! The goat ran away with it, munching up the sandwich AND the paper bag.

When we got to the cows, I was so hungry that I could have eaten one of them.

The cows were sitting down in the grass and looked very sleepy. One of my classmates, James, went up to one of them and patted her softly on her rump. He just wanted to find out what her fur felt like.

The cow was sitting there quietly, with

her tail lying in a pile of fresh poo behind her bottom.

But because the cow thought James' hand was like a fly on her skin, she wanted to shoo it away with her tail. She slapped James right in the forehead with her tail full of fresh sloppy cow poo.

All I heard was a chorus of EWWWWWW and YUUUUUUCK, but I thought it was a fantastic result.

Cow 1. James 0.

It was lunchtime, and I had nothing to eat because of the goat, so I grabbed a stick and started making dirt pictures. I wanted to move into a dirtier place, but then I noticed a pile of dry cow pats just lying there, so I put them to use by spinning them on my stick.

"WHO'S READY FOR A ROUND OF COWPAT DISCUS?"

I only heard one familiar voice, the voice of Patrick.

"I'll beat you any time, Slop!"

So, it was game on.

Patrick got himself a stick, and I had my go first; I could hear bystanders yelling:

"IS IT A BIRD? IS IT A PLANE? NO, IT'S A FLYING COWPAT, LOOK OUT!"

My cow pat went so far that it went over the fence and almost hit a grazing bull in the next yard.

"HA, I CAN BEAT THAT!"

Patrick flung his cowpat over the fence. He climbed on the top rail to see where his cowpat had landed, but all he could see was the raging bull coming at him.

WOOOOOM

"AAAAAHHHHHH"

Obviously, the bull didn't like Patrick. I can't blame him.

The bull had hit the fence with so much force that Patrick toppled over backward and landed in a new, fresh icky cow poo pat.

Everyone shrieked with laughter.

"Good on you!"

"That was worth a gold medal!"

"Hurray, first place!"

Dillon had a better idea to make use of the cowpats

"Let's play Dodge-Frisbee with the cow pats!"

I thought it was a great idea, so I flung one at him, and he got coated in dry cow pat pieces.

So, he flung one back at me and hit me

in the mouth with it. That made my already wobbly tooth wobble even more. The dry cow poo tasted like nothing.

Twenty minutes later, the bathrooms were filled with cow pat infested kids, but I got pulled out to come and talk to Patrick's mum.

"What do you have to say for yourself!?"

"It's not my fault! I wasn't the one who annoyed the bull!"

I didn't listen to the rest of what Patrick's mum was saying.

It had been a fun day, AND it had been a day of NEW messiness.

A great success.

All I was wondering now was what I could do with my wobbly tooth on the bus.

THE MYSTERY OF THE MISSING TOOTH

I kept wobbling my tooth with my tongue because I didn't want to touch it with my cow poo hands, and there were no basins on the bus.

When we got back to school, I gathered up all my stuff and headed for the exit of the bus. Mum was there to pick me up. The first thing that I heard was:

"Poo-Wee, what is that smell!?"

I kept wobbling my tooth for the whole evening, but it didn't come out.

I woke up the next morning — it was STILL THERE! I tried wobbling it some more, but it wouldn't budge. It was Saturday, so that meant that I had another school soccer game, but I didn't have a game plan because I was too focused on my tooth. I ended up getting substituted in the second half because I was not doing anything right.

After the game, Dad drove me home,

and on our way there, I decided that I was going to do something drastic with my tooth. I had a plan.

Mum and Dad were cleaning out the garage, so I saw this as an opportunity to get my tooth out. I went to the kitchen and opened the drawer where mum kept her ball of kitchen string. She keeps it to roll up meat for roasting it 'in a nice shape' as she calls it.

I cut off a long piece of string and strolled off to the bathroom. In front of the mirror, I attached one end of the string to my tooth and then went to get Grump.

I took Grump to the living room and sat him down in the middle of the carpet.

Should I go through with this? It could take more than one tooth out. What would I look like then? Would there be a lot of blood? I don't like the look of blood, and especially my blood.

I sat there on the carpet with Grump, the string hanging from my tooth.

I imagined what I would look like after the tooth was out and decided to get on with my plan.

I attached the other end of the string to Grump's collar and aimed him to the hallway. I opened my mouth a bit.

"Go, Grump! GOOOOO!"

I held on to the sofa, and Grump took off down the hallway taking my tooth with him. It was out!

The good news was I got my tooth out. The bad news was Grump kept running up and down the hallway and the living room, screeching to a halt every now and then. I told him to stop.

I first looked at Grump to see that the string was still attached to his collar, but on the other end of the string, the tooth wasn't there.

I looked around the carpet, but it had vanished!

Now what? I need my tooth. How will the tooth fairy believe I lost a tooth and give me a two-dollar coin if there is no evidence of a tooth?

I must find it!

THE VACUUM CLEANER!

I rushed to the laundry and dragged it out in the hope of finding my tooth. I vacuumed the living room and the hallway and then took the vacuum cleaner to the kitchen.

I got a pair of scissors and got out the vacuum cleaner bag and cut it open. Everything fell out on the kitchen floor. I didn't know we had that much dust in our house.!

I took a fork and sifted through

everything.

The good news was I found my tooth; the bad news was Grump came over intrigued to see whether I had found something interesting for him to eat.

He sniffed around in the pile of dust and sneezed five times:

"AAAAACHOOOO,
HEEECHOOOOO,
RACCHOOOO,
CHOOOOOOO,
RRRRRRRREEECHOOOOO!"

Because he is such a big dog, his sneezes were humongous. The last two sneezes were SOOO enormous that he also farted at the same time.

The dirt from the vacuum cleaner bag flew in all different directions.

That made ME sneeze too.

"HAACHOOOHACHEEE,

HAAAAACHOOO!"

I decided to clean it all up, but I couldn't use the vacuum cleaner anymore because I had cut a hole in its bag.

So, I was sitting there, in the middle of the dust pile, with my sneezing dog, when Mum came into the kitchen.

OH NO! I bet you can guess what she was saying.

And I hadn't even tried to make a mess this   time.

CREEPY CRAWLIES

It's Spring now, and the principal, Mr. Flint, has organized the Spring school camp for all the Grade-4s. Honestly, I've had enough of buses, but there is no other way to get there.

I also could not think of anything that I could do there to make the world a messier place — too many rules.

Rule 1. Lights out 7:30 on the dot.

Rule 2. No sporting equipment in the cabins.

Rule 3. No wandering out at night.

Rule 4. No food in cabins.

Rule 5. Be kind to the other kids.

My least favorite rule was Rule number 2. I thought it was the harshest thing in the entire universe.

The camp is by the sea, and it has 13 wooden cabins. We don't know who's in our cabins until we get there. I hoped I get Cameron and Dillon in my cabin, but not Patrick or his friends

I was worried that Mum might have forgotten to pack my teddy bear. I don't want my friends to know that I am anxious without it if I can't have Grump with me. But there are no dogs allowed in the camp.

This time nobody threw up on the bus. When we arrived, we went to a fancy hall that was called the 'Meeting Room'. That's also where the teachers and helpers go to hang out.

There they told us who was in our cabin. I was so excited to hear that I was in a cabin with Dillon and Cameron. Well, there was also a fourth person, and that was Jack. He is the most hyperactive kid in school. I wasn't excited to be sleeping in a cabin with a hyperactive kid that always brings a million candies to camp.

Next, we had to go on a nature walk. I like going on nature walks, but this one was different from all other nature walks.

We ambled along the riverbank. I was enjoying it until I felt a weird sensation on my left arm and my legs. It felt like something was crawling up my body.

I tried to shake it off, but it seemed to be latching on harder. I then dared to have a look at what it was.

"EEEEEEEEHHHHHH

AHHHHHHHHHH

EEEEEEEEERRRRRRRRRRRR

WHAT ARE THESE THINGS?!"

"They're just leeches."

Mr. Mark calmly explained how leeches work.

"They live in damp vegetation and latch onto people when they come through on the path here.

I tried to flick them off, and sure enough,

some of them came off easily.

Then I had an idea.

Patrick was at the end of our group. I called out:

"Patrick, look what I found!"

I jumped into the long grass.

"What is it?"

Patrick followed me, and we went deeper and deeper into the long grass.

"I can't see it anymore."

By this time, I was sure Patrick was covered in an army of leeches.

Then I had another idea.

I rummaged around in my pocket and pulled out the zip lock bag with apple slices that Mum had packed for me. I put the apple slices in my other pocket for later.

I grabbed the leeches that were still hanging on to my arms and legs and put them into the zip lock bag. I then stomped a bit more on the wet grass, hoping that more leeches would find me.

But no luck. These leeches would have to do. I put some grass and wet leaves into the zip lock bag with the leaches and hid it in my pocket.

When we got back to camp, we had a little bit of free time, so I used it to store the zip lock bag with the leaches in my bag to take home and put in Isabelle's bed.

We had dinner at the campfire, and then it was lights out.

About ten minutes into bedtime, Jack burst open his candy bag, and when he had finished with those, let's just say nobody got any sleep. I decided to get my pillow and sleep outside the cabin.

PIANO KEYS

The next morning, I felt terrible. I had mosquito bites all over me. They even bit me through my pajamas. I went to the toilets to inspect the damage.

I had red blotches all over me. Hundreds of them!

Cameron and Dillon made me count the mosquito bites. There were 38 of them, all red and ugly. All this counting made me go to breakfast about ten minutes late.

When I got there, there were no pancakes left. A big spoonful of maple syrup was all I needed to give me energy. I was lucky I did because we had to go on a 2-kilometer walk to a canoeing site.

At first, I was excited to go canoeing, but then again, a 2-kilometer walk is quite a long way.

When I got there, I could hardly move my feet, but on the bright side, I got Cameron as my canoeing partner.

Once I stepped into the canoe, I started to feel a bit nervous. It moved under my feet like nothing I've experienced before. I was worried I was going to fall into the water. The water did not look very appetizing, more reason not to fall in.

I sat down in the canoe with Cameron. We took the paddles in our hands, and one of the helpers pushed us out onto the river. That's when our problem started. The fin of my paddle fell off, and I only had a stick in my hand. We were slowly moving around in a small circle because Cameron had no idea how to steer with one paddle. One of the helpers had to row back to shore and get us a new paddle.

It was a windy day, and all the canoes started to drift away. We were left stranded there in the middle of the river.

Eventually, we got a new paddle, and we paddled to the other canoes that were waiting for us.

We decided to play 'Piano Keys' and if

you don't already know what 'Piano Keys' is, here are the rules.

First, you need to line up all the canoes together side by side into a kind of raft. They had already done that when we finally got to them.

Secondly, you need to stand up and get out of your own canoe and step on the nose of the next one.

Thirdly, you must run along the noses of all the canoes without falling into the water.

And finally, you must jump off the last canoe into the murky river.

The others had already started the game, and now it was my turn.

I stood up SLOWLY in my canoe. It wobbled a bit.

"Go on, Spickster! Hope you don't get sick from all the thin air up there!"

That was Patrick, of course.

"At least I won't sink like a big toad!" I replied.

I started running and jumping higher and higher from canoe to canoe. When I got to Patrick's, I had enough energy to put in a humungous jump that tipped the nose of his boat underwater.

Sure enough, he tried to rescue it by wobbling it to one side. He overdid it and tipped it over altogether. Like a cannonball, he flew in a nice curve, first up and then down, right into the river.

The splash was bigger than I had anticipated.

At the end of my run, I made it to the last canoe without falling in and jumped off.

I got covered from my toes to my forehead, but when I poked my head up out of the water, I yelled out at Patrick, who spewed river water out of his mouth.

"Hey, toad! How's it down there? Any rocks in the river to hide under?"

I could see that the canoes were slowly drifting away. I started to swim as fast as I could to the raft, and I managed to latch on to my canoe before it slipped away.

"You just wait!" Patrick didn't seem to be happy.

On our 2-kilometer walk back, I kept out of the way of the leeches. It was dinner time by then. This time it was lasagna, my favorite. I went back for seconds and thirds because I hadn't had any proper breakfast.

It was a great day. I was sorry that I hadn't found a way of getting messier than the others, but one day without extra mess was fine by me.

Fortunately, Jack had eaten all his candies on the first night, so we all had a good night's sleep.

BEACH BALL

The next morning, I got up bright and early, ready for breakfast. This time, we had bacon and eggs. I enjoyed that. I was all packed, ready to go home at lunchtime, but first, we did a beach walk.

Mr. Mark led the way. He showed us different types of seaweed. We also found shark eggs, and there were also a lot of dead starfish and tons and tons of mussel shells.

Patrick's mum was one of the helpers at camp.

"Don't get too wet, don't get into the water!"

What more did I need to know?

Wet? Water?

Cameron looked at me, I looked at him and Dillon, and we all nodded.

We walked as close as we could next to the waterline, and when a wave came in, we tried to race it up the beach. Of course, most of the time, the wave got us, and our shoes got wet.

After a while, we had our snack at the beach, and Mr. Mark allowed us free time to play on the beach.

We would have liked to play soccer, but nobody had brought any soccer balls. But then Cameron had an idea.

"Why don't we make soccer balls with seaweed?"

I thought it was a fantastic idea, so that's what we did. We rolled up strands of seaweed and knotted the balls together with thinner seaweeds. Each of us made three balls because we thought they would fall apart. They were quite heavy.

Cameron and I set up a small sand goal. We took turns at being goalie and kicking.

The balls flew up in the air towards the goal, but in the middle of the game, the soccer balls kept exploding, and we got covered from head to toe in sand and seaweed bits. It was like kicking with dead soccer balls filled with spaghetti.

THUDD

PLOP

ZMMMMM

DOMP.

One hit Dillon in the face. He got covered in seaweed, but he didn't mind.

My last ball flew into a wave, and I went to get it. Unfortunately, I tripped on a plastic bottle and fell into the water. The ball was gone.

Cameron won by two points, but we all had fun.

I was dripping wet, covered in seaweed and sand from head to toe. Not dirt — but enough stuff that mum would find horrid.

I squished one of the soccer balls into

my snack pack to take home. Mr. Mark had used seaweed fertilizer for the school garden. I would make some fertilizer to fertilize our lawn at home. Mum always says I am ruining it with my soccer skill training.

When we got to school, Mum was there to pick me up. I could hear her muttering to herself.

"Errrr! Yuck! Disgusting!"

With all the salty beach smell coming from my clothes and snack pack, with sand and seaweed in my shoes and the leaches in my pocket, I think I had a pretty good time at camp.

While mum put my clothes into the wash, I took out my zip lock bag to release the leaches into Isabelle's bed.

OH, NO!

They had all shriveled up and died

amongst the grass and leaves. Not even one was still alive.

I had to think of new ways of getting on with my job of being the messiest kid at home and school.

Tomorrow I would do something with the seaweed, which I had hidden in the garage.

A GREAT PAINT JOB

On Sunday, Cameron came with us to

the last Golden Square District Soccer Club game of the season. He practiced soccer skills on the sidelines until Owen and I had finished our match. Dad bought us hamburgers because he said Mum didn't need to cook today.

Back at home, we went into our garage to put the seaweed into a bucket of water to turn it into fertilizer. Mum and dad had cleaned out the garage, but our old toy boxes were still there.

I looked at them. Maybe we could find something to play with that was different from the games we had now.

"Here, this is something we could try." Owen pulled out a box of acrylic craft paints. There were quite a lot of used tubes of green, blue, yellow, red, black, and white, and a few brushes too.

"Oh yes, I remember this. We used to do finger-painting with this."

On the box, it said: 'Water-based acrylic craft paint'. But there was no paper to paint on.

"What can we do with this?"

"Obviously, we can't paint on the walls."

"Unfortunately."

Cameron's eyes lit up.

"We could paint each other and then wash it off again before dinner."

"Great idea."

We took the box and brushes to the lawn and took our clothes off, except our shorts.

It was a lovely sunny day, and we were not cold.

First, I squeezed a bit of red paint on a brush and drew a line on Cameron's nose, from between his eyes right down to the tip.

"Looks like war paint!"

He took another brush and painted a blue dot on my back. Owen squeezed green paint on his left hand and then smeared it on Cameron's back, all over his shoulder blades. Nice.

That worked quicker than the brushes. We all used the paint tubes now to spread colors over our bodies. With the brushes, we painted rings around our eyes.

We used a different color scheme for each of us. I was mostly black and yellow like a wasp, Cameron was red and blue on his chest and the front of his legs, with bright green and white dots on his back. Owen was mostly black on the back, and green and blue on his front. He had drawn white bones all down his legs. He looked like a skeleton.

Eventually, we ran out of paint.

"We need to take a picture of this."

I ran into the house through the laundry into my room to get my mobile phone.

We took pictures of each other, and then we decided it was time to wash the paint off. We were getting hungry again — time to get inside and find something to eat.

I turned on the garden tap and started hosing down Owen.

What was this? Only the paint that we put on last and that hadn't dried yet came off. All the dried paint stayed on. Cameron tried to hose himself off — the same result.

I started panicking.

"Oh, No. What do we do now? How can we get this off?"

We went into the garage to find something to dissolve the paint with but no luck. At least there were some old rags, and we used them to try and rub the paint off. It worked a little bit, but not enough.

I called Dad on his mobile phone.

"Dad, can you please come into the garage. We need your help with something."

"Sure, wait a sec, I will be there in a tic."

When Dad saw us, he started laughing. He gasped and coughed and slapped his thighs.

"I can't believe my eyes. This is hilarious. This stuff will stick to you for weeks. Let me take a picture of you three geniuses. I will send it to your parents, Cam."

"We can't get it off. It said it is water-based, but it doesn't wash off. Can you get it off us somehow before Mum finds out?"

"This is more difficult than you think. Water-based means that the paint color is mixed into a water base, so it stays soft until you use it with a brush. Once the water has evaporated, and the paint is dry, it won't come off anymore. It gives you just enough time to wash off your brushes and wash it off your hands before it dries. It's not meant for painting bodies."

I started to cry.

"Do we have to go to school like this?"

"I'll try my best to get it off. Let's go inside and see if we can rub most of it off with a sponge under warm water."

Dad pushed us inside through the laundry door and into the bathroom.

"Let's start with your faces so we can get most of that paint off first. What stays on your body can be covered by your clothes tomorrow."

Dad gave us a handful of face washers and the brush that Mum uses for scrubbing the dishes. He filled the bathtub with warm water

"Get in and scrub, scrub, scrub! Stop scrubbing when the paint is off — or your skin comes off." He grinned and walked out.

We worked hard at scrubbing ourselves and each other. It took a lot of effort and a long time to get our faces clean. Owen's fake bones came off easily because he had painted them last, but the blue dot on my back and the green smear on Cameron's shoulder blades did not budge. They became a little bit fainter, but they did not disappear. The worst color to get off was the black paint.

Our bathwater had turned into a murky grey-brown color. We had to change it three times.

Dad shoved a pile of towels and dry clothes through the door.

"Come out when you are done. Let's have some hot chocolate afterward. Mum has made an apple crumble. She will be so happy to see you all clean and shiny."

Eventually, we had to get out of the bathtub because no more paint came off. What was left on us had to grow out by itself.

We came into the kitchen, quiet like little lambs.

Mum gave us each a plate with apple crumble and a mug with hot chocolate.

We planted ourselves in front of the TV and watched the Lego movie.

All in all, a great day, but my skin hurt all over from all the scrubbing.

I decided to give a miss to messiness tomorrow — or until my skin stopped hurting.

DOG SALON

School was getting boring except that Patrick put a bunch of slaters into my lunchbox.

Great trick, Patrick. Slaters are harmless and don't do anything. They just look ugly. I shook them off from my crustless sandwich and took a big bite out of it. I pretended that this was the most delicious sandwich of all time.

Everyone was watching.

"Gross."

"Revolting!"

"Disgusting."

"This is SOOOO sick."

After school, Mum had gone shopping, and Isabelle was hiding in her room, having some secret conversations on her mobile.

I took Grump to the park, and we had a good time playing with sticks.

But then Grump got side-tracked and started sniffing and pawing at a patch of grass. He paused and seemed to think about what to do next.

He slowly put his head down to make sure he had found the right spot and started rolling on that patch of grass, not only once but several times.

When I walked over to him, he had some greenish slime all over his shoulders and neck. It looked like vomit, and it smelled disgusting, like something dead.

According to Mum, dogs are dirt magnets and need to be washed all the time. She takes Grump to the Dog Salon every couple of weeks for a wash and every three months for a hair trim. I think it is a waste of money to pay for a dog salon if we have a perfectly good shower to do it ourselves.

I took Grump home straight away to get this stuff off his fur. I locked in the garage so I could get organized. His smell was so foul it made me feel like vomiting, but he didn't seem to mind it at all.

I first prepared the shower in Mum and Dad's bathroom that goes off from their bedroom. There is a beautiful light grey soft carpet on the floor in their bedroom, and the bathroom tiles are also very light grey. I think Mum chose that color because you can see every tiny speck of dirt on it with your naked eye.

I put the bottle of shampoo onto the shower floor to have it handy and three towels next to the shower. I then got undressed to my undies before I took the dog lead off the hook in the hallway to get Grump.

Grump looked at me with suspicious eyes.

"Why does he wear no clothes now? What is he up to? Surely he is not taking me for a walk again?"

I led Grump into the bathroom and pulled him into the shower. I kept hold of the lead and closed the glass door.

Even though he usually likes playing at the beach or in mud puddles, he did not like the idea of being in the shower.

First, I made him wet all over with warm water before I put shampoo all over him and more water to make the soap distribute better.

I then used my fingers to wash his fur. I tried to make lots of bubbles to cover up the smell and the looks of the mess.

GRAAAAARAWWW! That gunk felt disgusting, slimy, and it still stank.

Grump did not like it one bit.

He tried to escape, and I tried to keep hold of him with my legs and hands and the dog leash. That did not work out for me. I slipped and had to let go of everything.

Because he is SOOO BIG, he just fell out through the shower door that opened when he pushed on it.

Oh, NOOOO!

Of course, he was out like a flash and did not want to be caught again.

Soap dripped off him in little waterfalls and foam balls.

Because I was all soapy from Grump and he was even soapier, we both made a gigantic frothy slimy mess all through the house while chasing after each other.

Grump jumped on the sofa.

He jumped on Isabelle's bed.

He jumped on my bed – which I didn't mind much.

He jumped back into Isabelle's bed and burrowed under her doona.

When I tried to grab him, he slid out at the foot end of her bed and ran along the corridor into the kitchen.

Eventually, I thought that this was getting out of hand a bit too much.

I opened the door to the lawn to let him out.

PHEEW!

Grump ran outside and threw himself on the lawn. He slid along and rolled and rolled all over to get the soap off him. Obviously, he also preferred to be messy rather than clean.

I left him there and went inside to clean up a bit. I thought Mum would probably find this mess a little too big for her liking.

I got a new doona cover for Isabelle's

doona and put it over the dirty one. It looked beautiful and clean.

Next, I took a towel and tried to clean the wet soapy footprints from the sofa. But the patches got bigger from wiping them. I gave up and rearranged the cushions, so it was not so obvious.

The worst part was cleaning up the carpet in Mum and Dad's bedroom, where Grump's and my footprints were super-wet and sloshy. I tried to soak the water up with the towels, but it did not work very well.

Because all of Grump's dirt had gone into the shampoo on his body and had run down his legs, his footprints had turned dark brown.

This mess was gigantic. Even though I wanted to be the biggest dirt magnet ever, I had probably created the biggest mess in the history of the universe.

I felt a little bit worried about Mum and Dad finding out before I could fix it to a level that could hide most of it.

"Oh, NO!"

I heard mum unlocking the front door.

"She is home from shopping! Grump! Stay Outside! Don't come in PLEASE!"

But what does Grump do?

Bounce, Bounce, Bounce! Here he comes running into the house — right up to Mum, his tail wagging.

"EEEEEEEEK!!!!"

Mum takes one step forward and slips on the soapy floor.

She throws her arms up; the shopping bags go flying in the air.

CRASH!

BANG — BANG — BANG!

"OUCH! My Back!"

Mum sits on the floor, looking around with eyes like saucers.

I know I am in trouble.

I am not going to go into the "discussions" Mum and Dad unloaded on me. Too detailed but words like 'irresponsible', 'feral', 'stupid', were part of this DISCUSSION.

"We need to get a carpet cleaner in to fix the carpets and the sofa."

"I agree," said Dad.

I got banned for one month from all technology and from playing FIFA 18.

I cannot recommend this method of creating a mess if your dog is bigger and stronger than you or if the punishment you will receive for messing up the house is bigger than you want to experience. Like missing out for four weeks on FIFA 18. That was too much. A whole month for washing the dog and accidentally creating a mess — which was not really meant to happen at all.

Mum banished Grump to the laundry for the night. I felt sorry for him, and when everyone was asleep, I took my pillow and doona to the laundry, and we both slept in the dog bed together. It was a bit tight, but we kept each other warm.

PART THREE

While I was listening to Grump's snoring, I started thinking.

Is this really what I was hoping to achieve when I had made my decision to become super-messy?

My goal had been to have more control over my life. Have I achieved that now? Lying here in Grump's dog bed did not feel like being in control of anything.

I had hoped that Mum would accept that a little bit of dirt won't hurt. But had I managed to convince her of that?

Did my friends at school like me more now since I had become a dirt magnet? And most of all, had Patrick stopped teasing me?

I had to admit to myself that the answer to every one of these questions was 'NO'.

What should I do?

I felt tears coming up in my eyes and used one of Grump's ears to wipe them off. No point in thinking about it more now. Grump licked my face, and after a little while, we fell asleep.

WHAT TO DO ABOUT MATT?

In the morning, Mum was still angry, and Dad ignored me. I kept a low profile. I was tired, and I smelled like a dog, but Mum didn't say anything about that.

At school, I found that nobody wanted to be around me.

"You stink."

Patrick gave me a shove.

"Haven't you got water at home?"

Lisa sniffed at me.

"Our dog smells better than you. In fact, everything smells better than you."

My skin still had a grey tint from the acrylic paint from the weekend.

"What's the matter with you? Are you living under your house now instead of in it?"

"Are you practicing becoming a chimney

sweep now? I thought you want to be a soccer player."

I didn't say anything. I had wanted to be messy so that everyone could see that I was like everyone else. But obviously, everyone still thought I was not like everyone else. And maybe I had turned into a creature that everyone liked even less than before.

They didn't call me 'Spick' anymore. They didn't call me 'Messy'. They didn't call me anything. They just didn't want to hang around me.

Mum had packed my lunch as usual, but this time, she had not cut the crusts. At least one positive thing today. I ate it by myself, near the guinea pig hutch.

When Mum picked me up from school, she had Grump in the car. She had taken him to the dog grooming salon, and they had clipped all his fur off, except on his head, which still looked fluffy. He looked skinny without his big fur coat, and he smelt like a flower shop. He looked at me with sad eyes, and we cuddled up together in the back of the car. Neither he nor I said anything.

On the way home, Mum gave me a lecture about my behavior.

"Obviously, you have decided to turn yourself into a revolting feral thug without manners — a shame to yourself and your family. I try my hardest to keep you in a presentable state and make sure that you become a responsible person. I have decided to take you to a counselor to find out what is wrong with you. I will make an appointment for tomorrow so we can get to the bottom of this as fast as possible. But first, I will talk to your teacher to find out whether you have slipped in your schoolwork too."

I sank deeper into the back seat and hugged Grump even tighter.

What now? Somehow everything had gone wrong since I had started on my journey to become a super-messy dirt magnet. And most of the time, I hadn't even tried my hardest to create a mess. It had happened all by itself without much trying.

At home, I went outside and practiced my soccer skills on the lawn, but even that did not make me happy today. I couldn't get them right, and the ball slipped off my feet most times.

After dinner, I brushed my teeth and went to bed. I waited until everyone had gone to bed and then got Grump from the laundry. I let him sleep in my bed under my blanket to keep warm.

A CHAT ABOUT DIRT

In the morning, Dad still ignored me. I brushed my teeth and my hair and washed my face and hands before getting into the car.

Dad dropped us off at school as usual.

"Have a great day!"

Isabelle walked off with her friends. She didn't want to be seen with me.

I felt like an outcast of the worst kind. Not even my family likes me anymore.

During recess, Mr. Mark came over to me while I was eating my fruit snack.

He sat down next to me.

Oh no, I thought. Mum must have talked to him already.

"What seems to be the trouble, Matt?"

"Trouble? Nothing much."

"Hmm, I don't quite believe you." He looked me in the eyes.

"I notice you have been taking much less care with your appearance lately. The other kids don't want to be around you anymore, and they make fun of you because of that. What is the reason for all of this? Your locker is a mess, your schoolbag is a mess, your hair is a mess most days, and you look a bit grubby all over. Why is that? You can tell me. I won't tell anyone else. Maybe we can work it all out."

At first, I didn't want to tell him why I had started to become messy, but the words just flowed out of my mouth like a flood of ants.

I told him that the kids had made fun of me because I was so super-tidy and spotless and that I wanted to be like them. Just ordinary with ordinary dirt on me, like them. But then it all got out of hand, and my messiness had turned into disasters. The kids liked me even less now, and Mum wanted to take me to a counselor.

I almost started crying. I blinked hard and did not know what to say next.

"I see." He made a long pause. "I think this problem can be fixed quite easily."

I looked up, hoping that easy meant that it would also be fast. I felt that my life was more out of control now than before I started on my journey of becoming super-messy. I waited for Mr. Mark to speak.

"You like our Enviro-Science projects, don't you?"

I nodded.

"You have seen the weeds in the vegetable garden and the soccer pitch. And there are some in the orchard."

I nodded again. I hadn't seen the weeds in the soccer pitch, but I had seen the others. Mr. Mark continued to speak.

"We rip out the weeds because we want the vegetables to grow better. But how do we know which plants are weeds? How do we decide what's a weed and what is not?"

"I don't know. You tell us which plants to pull out because they are weeds."

"Yes, but how do I know what a weed is?

I shrugged my shoulders. I had never thought about that before.

"A weed is a plant that grows in the wrong place. That is all."

"Really?"

"Yes. Think about it. A thistle plant in the soccer pitch is not a bad plant. It is just a plant in the wrong place. Grass in the vegetable garden bed is not a bad plant. It is a good plant — in a cow pasture for cows to eat. But it is a plant in the wrong place in a garden bed. You get it?"

I nodded. Why did he tell me all this? What did weeds have to do with me?

"Now that you understand weeds, you can understand what dirt is. Dirt is a substance in the wrong place."

It dawned on me that he might be right.

Maybe there is no dirt. Just stuff in the wrong place. Like mud on me instead of in a mud puddle. Paint on my body instead of on a piece of paper — mud in the dog fur or on the carpet instead of outside where it usually belongs. Maybe ketchup in Owen's hair is also stuff in the wrong place. Maybe dirt didn't belong in my ears. Neither did slugs belong in a birdcage. They belonged outside.

"I think I understand."

"There is a reason why things should be

in their correct place. If everything is put in places where they don't belong, life becomes very unpredictable.

You never can know 100 percent in advance what will happen if you put something in the wrong place. Something might happen that you don't expect."

I nodded. I could see that. I had not expected that putting Grump into the shower or making soapy footprints would cause so much chaos.

"If too many people put stuff in the wrong place all the time, life becomes chaos. That is why we have rules. Rules about school uniforms and behavior. For no other reason."

I nodded.

"I heard you are a very decent soccer player on the A-team. Is it true you want to be like Lionel Messi?"

I nodded again.

"Soccer has rules, about how to play the game, how to behave, and what to wear. Imagine Lionel Messi would turn up in a Juventus top instead of an FC Barcelona top to a match. Would his team respect him if he turned up to practice smelling like a dog? I think not.

I think you understand the message. If you try to be messier than you usually get doing ordinary things, you are just trying to get attention. Attention for the wrong reason, and from the wrong people."

"But how can I stop my Mum from treating me like a baby and keep me so mollycoddled that everyone laughs at me and teases me for being super clean?"

"Tell your parents how you feel about it and that it does not help. They will understand that their future soccer player son needs to pack his healthy school lunches every day. Show them that you can take responsibility for your appearance and your own stuff. I am sure they will come around to it if you try it for a week or two. Show them you can do it without chaos."

The bell went, and we both got up.

IS IT REALLY THAT EASY?

I kept thinking about what Mr. Mark had said. I kept out of the way of the other kids for the rest of the day.

After the last bell, we had soccer practice again. I worked my heart out to get my skills right and pass the ball more often than I usually do. I got praise from our coach.

"Well done today. I see you have woken up from your deep sleep during the last few weeks. Keep up the good work."

I was chuffed.

"Remember, on Saturday, you will be at the school championships. You are very close to having the highest goal-scoring points of all teams. So, focus, focus, focus!"

When Dad picked me up from school that day, I said to him that I was sorry for being such a moron for the last few weeks and creating so much chaos at home. He nodded.

"It's okay."

"Can you please tell Mum that I want to pack my own gear every day for school and my school lunch box too. I am not a baby anymore. People are laughing at me at school because I have the crusts cut off my sandwiches. Please, can you?

I will try and look after my stuff and try and stand up for myself. I promise not to make more mess than what happens just by accident."

Dad nodded.

"Hopefully, there will also be less dog mess in the future."

"Yes, I will look after him better. I promise."

That night, I had a proper shower and cut my toenails.

The next morning, Mum had lined up bread and cheese and other things on the kitchen bench, so I could make my lunch box. It took me a while, but I got it done in time. She did not brush my hair before I went out the door, and she did not check whether I had brushed my teeth.

My life is getting better, I thought.

Mum drove us to school that morning. When we got there, and I started walking towards class, I remembered I had forgotten something. I turned around and ran back to give Mum a big hug. Both of our days were getting better.

When Patrick called me names at school that day, I ignored him. I thought calling me names is like putting words into the wrong place. They were like weeds, just in the wrong place, nothing more. I decided to keep them out of my ears and out of my mind.

I kept thinking of Saturday. How could I kick more goals for our school team?

At recess, I practiced again with Dillon

and Cameron. After a little while, Zoe came over and asked whether she could play too. She is on the girls' team.

"Sure." We all said.

THE BIG GAME

The big day! The day of the match that will go down in history as Meadow Vale Middle School's most memorable match ever. A-team versus B-team!

I could feel my stomach going around and around like it was being tossed about in a washing machine. Dillon felt the same. On the other hand, Cameron was pumped. He was so ready for the game of his life.

"You ready?" an encouraging voice said.

I was looking around and saw a shadow coming closer to me from the main hall. Cameron and Dillon were already waiting for me at the sidelines, but I turned to get closer to the shadow.

It turned out to be Mr. Mark.

"Are you ready?"

"You bet I am!" I replied rapidly

"Matt! C'mon!" Yelled another voice.

"Oh, I'd better go."

"Well, have fun then!" said Mr. Mark

My heart was racing a million miles an hour, as Cameron kicked the ball to Dillon on the wing. Our team darted to the ball like bees to honey. About 5 minutes into the match, Cameron shot the ball from 15 meters out, and it hit the crossbar. Everyone stopped and froze. Then Patrick, the B-team goalie, pounced from his goal, but I just reached the ball in time to push it with my toe away from Patrick's gloves and it into the goal.

"GOAL!" Yelled the teachers and parents on the sidelines, as our team celebrated. I even could hear Dad's voice. We were in the lead.

1–0.

Patrick was now fuming. He was jumping up and down, and then he booted the ball into the crowd.

In the second half, Dillon was running up the wing, and then he crossed the ball to the middle. It flew majestically through the air. Cameron jumped up. The ball clipped his head and shot into the top left corner of the goal.

2–0.

"HOORAY!"

The B-team swarmed toward our goal, like a stampede of angry bulls. Our goalie was petrified. One of the opposition players shot the ball into the bottom right corner of our goal.

2–1.

The crowd was on their toes when the big bulky defender on the B-team charged up the field toward our goal. I could not out-sprint him, and so he used all his force to rocket the ball into the back of our net.

2–2.

Our team was shocked, and Patrick was

jumping up and down again, calling out at the top of his voice:

"HOORAY!"

"LOSERS!"

I turned to Patrick and then sprinted up the field. I called out for the ball.

"Here, give me the ball!"

Cameron passed it to me. I had my back to Patrick, who had come out of his goal. Big mistake! He was coming up behind me.

I could feel his breath at the back of my head and ran faster to get some space and turn around towards the goal.

BANG!

My legs were kicked out from under me. I fell flat on my belly, and my face hit the grass. Patrick had done it again.

"TOOT" went the whistle.

"FOUL!"

I stood up, and I shook my head. I looked around and noticed that my whole class was watching, including Mr. Mark.

The referee placed the ball down on the shiny white penalty dot — in the last minute of the match. It was now or never.

Patrick was now hopping up and down, again, shouting:

"SPICK!"

"POND-WORM!"

"LOSER, YOU WILL MISS THIS!"

"YOU ARE THE WORST SOCCER PLAYER EVER!"

He was trying to put me off, but I knew

that these words were like weeds in my brain. I chucked them out and focused on where I would kick the ball.

I looked at the top right corner of the goal, with hope in my eyes. I tried to stay calm, even though my legs were shaking.

I slowly retracted my left foot and booted the ball as hard as I could. I almost missed it, but it curved off to the left, instead of to the right, and went in the top left corner.

I did it!

The result was 3–2!

"TOOT — TOOT — TOOT"

The end of the game!

HOORAY

HOORAY

Everyone jumped up and down, screaming at the top of their voice. Our team hugged, and we all fell over the top of each other on the soccer pitch.

The parents and teachers cheered from the sidelines.

"Well done!"

"Super!"

I could see Dad punching holes in the air.

We all lined up after the game and, after a break, the principal gave out the awards for the season. There were awards for everything, best and fairest, for both the girls' and the boys' teams, best goalie, and others.

Cameron got an award as the boys' best and fairest. I patted him on the back.

Patrick did not win 'best goalie'. He pretended he didn't care, but I could see he was mad. He kicked the grass so hard that it came out of the ground, roots and all, when he did not get called.

I was only interested in the highest goal scorer award and couldn't wait for it to be announced.

"And now to the award for the highest goal scorer of the season!"

I was hopping up and down on the spot.

"In third place James McDonald."

"In second place, Dillon Brown."

"And in first place…"

"MATT ……"

I did not hear the rest of what the principal said. I ran up to him to get my trophy and held it up in the air.

My dream had come true. I had become the Lionel Messi of our school.

THE END
(for now)

ABOUT THE AUTHOR

Cam R. Pearce lives on a small farm in a small country town in Victoria, Australia, with his mum, dad, and sister. He loves playing soccer, the violin, Minecraft, and watching YouTube videos. When he is not glued to technology, he races around on his bicycle and plays with his dog Roxie and the four family cats.

Made in United States
North Haven, CT
08 June 2022